The End We Start From

MEGAN HUNTER

The End We Start From

PICADOR

First published 2017 by Picador
an imprint of Pan Macmillan
20 New Wharf Road, London N1 9RR
Associated companies throughout the world
www.panmacmillan.com

ISBN 978-1-5098-3910-0

1 3 5 7 9 8 6 4 2

A CIP catalogue record for this book is available from the British Library.

Printed and bound by CPI Group (UK) Ltd, Croydon, CR0 4YY

For my mother and my son.

What we call the beginning is often the end
And to make an end is to make a beginning.
The end is where we start from.

T. S. Eliot, *Four Quartets*

The End We Start From

i.

I am hours from giving birth, from the event I thought would never happen to me, and R has gone up a mountain.

When I text him, he sends his friend S to look after me, and starts down the mountain.

S is scared, and has brought J.

J is also scared, and has brought beer.

They watch me from a corner of the room as though I am an unpredictable animal, a lumbering gorilla with a low-slung belly and suspicious eyes. Occasionally they pass me a banana.

They try to put *Match of the Day* on. I growl. I growl more and more, and finally I am waterless, the pool of myself spreading slowly past my toes.

They flap like small birds around the water, they perch on my giant head, they speak of kettles and hot towels.

I tell them I have to push, and they back away, reaching for their phones.

* * *

At first there was only the sea, only the sky. From the sky came a rock, which dropped deep into the sea. A thick slime covered the rock, and from this slime words grew.

* * *

Before I dilate, we agree: R will get his two nights in nature. He will climb and trek, camp and forage.

I am nearly as wide as I am tall. In the supermarket, people avoid me. Sometimes, in narrow hallways, I get stuck.

All by itself, the head balls into place.

* * *

We have planned a water birth, with whale music, and hypnotism, and perhaps even an orgasm.

My usual cynicism has been chased away by the fear of pain, of losing control, of all things bloody and stretching.

The moment of birth looms ahead of me like the loss of my virginity did, as death does. The inevitable, tucked and waiting out there somewhere.

Once, when I was about eight, I looked at a telegraph pole as hard as I could. I made a mind-photo, urged myself to remember it that night.

When I did, the rest of the day seemed like it had never happened. I terrified myself that I would do this at the moment of death, that I could trick my whole life away.

When I was a child I thought I had been chosen for our times. The ending times. The creeping times.

* * *

I am thirty-two weeks pregnant when they announce it: the water is rising faster than they thought. It is creeping faster. A calculation error. A badly plotted movie, sensors out at sea.

We hide under the duvet with a torch like children. I ask R if he still would have done it. If he had known. He doesn't answer.

He shines the torch up into the duvet and makes his fingers into ducks. I decide to take that as a yes.

* * *

I am a geriatric primigravida, but I don't look it.

We have leather sofas. R spills takeaway on them and grins: wipe clean.

I am thirty-eight weeks when they tell us we will have to move. That we are within the Gulp Zone.

I say whoever thought of that name should be boiled in noodles. R spends all night on the same property website. It is loading very slowly.

* * *

Man came from a germ. From this germ he was fashioned, from clot to bones to thick flesh. He stood up on one end, a new creation.

* * *

J phones an ambulance and S looks out of the window palely.

I gaze at the wooden floor. I have never noticed how beautiful it is before.

It is perfectly dusk-coloured, and the whorls are rising like dark little planets through its glow.

Between the waves of disembowelling wrench the world is shining. I feel like Aldous Huxley on mescaline. I am drenched in is-ness.

* * *

When I am thirty-nine weeks they tell us we don't have to move, actually; it was all a mistake.

Pinch of salt, R grumbles, glancing at my belly.

* * *

R arrives four minutes after the boy is born, frowning and yellow, into the midwife's hands. I am too exhausted to hold him. My eyes ache from three hours of pushing. My undercarriage is a pulp.

* * *

In the darkness demons flew. Their shapes made a fearful noise until a voice called out, and they were still, and the silence was complete.

* * *

I am in the hospital when R comes to tell me, but I already know. The reports have spread through the ward like infection.

In the bed across from me a girl possibly just young enough to be my granddaughter cuddles her toddler on one side and her newborn on the other.

Schoolboys visit her and let their eyes roam over my udders as they pass.

I am veined and topless, doing skin to skin with the boy, who is mysterious and silent. Occasionally he twitches, as though remembering something.

In the night a nurse with hunched shoulders like the start of wings comes to my bedside and lifts him to me. She says his eyes look like sharks' eyes. They all do.

* * *

The lady through the curtain has no baby.

Or she has one, but he is upstairs in a plastic box filled with wires and tubes, and she wails out for more drugs.

Crash section, I hear the midwives murmuring. They give her the drugs.

She has a radio and doesn't use headphones. She has her pain and no baby so I don't say anything.

She likes talk radio mostly, interminable phone-ins in different accents that all pass through my body in the same way.

The phrases spill out, unstoppable. Deckchairs, document, pressure, response.

They seem to swell from under me like a bath filling up. Like indigestion. Like something no bad simile could ever do justice to.

* * *

I am eating lime jelly with the boy in the crook of my arm when I hear.

7

His hands circle in tiny, victorious fists. I feel that I could, all things considered, conquer the world.

The news on the hour, 14th June, one o'clock. Tina Murphy reporting. An unprecedented flood. London. Uninhabitable. A list of boroughs, like the shipping forecast, their names suddenly as perfect and tender as the names of children. Ours.

Two hours later R is there, breaking the news again, lifting the boy against his shoulder. Apologizing like it's his fault.

* * *

The hospital now seems to be a ship, a brightly lit ark housing all the new ones aloft.

We – the women in the open-backed gowns, bursting stitches in the bathroom – are their escorts.

The food becomes a lot worse.

ii.

They throw us out on the third day. I am barely intact but the boy is whole, completely made, crowned with a name that will carry him to his grave.

We nearly called him Noah, but we heard it rustling between the curtains. A popular choice.

I am incapable of original thought, so R takes it on, digs out the list we slaved over in another universe.

Tristan, Caleb, Alfred, he recites, whilst the boy sucks seriously on my still-empty breast.

Jonas, Gregor, Bob, he intones over the boy's sludge-filled nappies.

Percy, Woody, Zeb, he sings at the window. London swims out in front of him, darkly reflective. The boy jerks his head on the last syllable, and this decides it. Z we call him, ZZZZ we hum, hoping it will make him a sleeper.

* * *

We load Z into his high-tech protective car seat. We drive on the roads that are left.

R puts the Beach Boys on. We get around. We get out, somehow.

R learnt to drive on a farm. He finds tracks, dog-legs, narrow lanes where birds are singing.

* * *

Z sleeps all the way along the curved spine of the country, up into the mountains where R was born.

When we arrive, his mother runs from the house with her arms open.

* * *

In these days we shall look up and see the sun roaming

across the night and the grass rising up. The people will cry without end, and the moon will sink from view.

* * *

R's father N will not turn the television off. I stay in the kitchen, the only screenless room, with my smarting pulp on a cushion and the baby mushed against my breast.

R's mother G will not stop talking. This not-stopping seems to be the first side effect.

Everything has been unstopped, is rising to the surface.

* * *

On the third day up high, R starts building. There is a shed in the garden that he says we can live in, with a few modifications.

Z opens his eyes a little more every day. I am constantly aware of the complex process of breath: how the heart has to keep beating, to bring oxygen to the blood, to power the bags of the lungs in and out. Or something.

It seems that any moment it could stop. Sometimes he sleeps so quietly it seems that he has gone.

* * *

We mostly lie in R's old childhood bedroom, now with double bed and Moses basket creaking with Z's every move.

The news rushes past downstairs like a flow of traffic. Even our flat back there underwater doesn't make it real.

Z is real, with his tiny cat skull and sweet-smelling crap. The news is rushing by. It is easy to ignore.

* * *

Every morning when I wake up the sheets are wet. I have wet myself from my breasts; I am lying in milk. Z tosses and the wicker stirs. R is already out of bed. If I listen carefully enough I can hear him hammering in the garden.

Words float up the stairs like so many childhood letter magnets. Endgame, civilization, catastrophe, humanitarian.

When I go out in the garden with Z he opens his eyes under the trees and they are filled with clouds. I kiss his head and we watch R together. There is only a pile of planks at the bottom of the garden, no home.

* * *

The times I like are when N and R and sometimes G go out in the car for supplies. It takes hours, due to all the queues and shortages and fights. I am exempt, due to having Z and a healing body.

Sometimes Z sleeps on me while I read or watch a film (never news), sometimes he sleeps in his buggy (donated by neighbours) and I wash his yellow-streaked babygrows in the bathroom sink.

The crap floats down the plug like tiny beasts. The water flows over my hands, it flows into the sink. Z continues to breathe. There is no news. There is no hammering. These are the times that I like.

* * *

G will still not stop talking, but she is happy. She is happier than I have ever seen her before. She keeps saying it's like in the war, even though she has never been in any wars.

She likes making simple meals from simple things. She likes making the meat stretch through the whole week. When she says this I can only think of sinews pulled tight across the house, connecting the tap to the door handle, the chair to the fireplace.

I never used to know what to say to G, but now I pat Z's bottom and smile at her. He has given me a purpose.

* * *

So much of life these days is spent feeling that we are on a ship. After the hospital ship, the in-law ship, and the tiny cabin that has become our world.

R is building, but the pile of planks remains.

* * *

The day they don't come back from shopping is beautiful: sun through green leaves and the baby getting visibly fat.

I have warmed soup, and when the clock gets late I push the pot to the back of the stove.

I sing to Z. I watch the sky dim and switch off.

We go to bed. Instead of putting him in his basket I lay him next to me, and fall asleep with my nose pressed against his pulsing temple.

* * *

And on that day the wind will rush through the fields like a reckoning, and the mothers will hold their children, and the shepherds will lose their sheep.

* * *

In the morning things are empty and strange, like camping used to be. I have started to think of myself as a bear, with my young clinging to my neck, when I hear the car.

R and N climb out slowly. There is no G. They come into the house like soldiers, like fading people from an old photo.

No G.

* * *

A tea towel in the back of the car, a crumple of pastel birds. One of her favourites.

A few ashamed-looking packets in the boot, lying at angles, their sides touching, just.

* * *

R and N sit in the house like they've never seen it before. I prop Z on my shoulder, and make tea like you're supposed to. I stir piles of sugar in.

Too many, R says. Too little.

Pandemonium, N tries, syllables spilling onto the table.

G is nowhere, and the kitchen is full of her, her face shining out from the kettle, the shape of her waist wrapped around jars.

They stare at the tea. R blows his. Neither of them drinks.

iii.

Z has learnt to smile. He has cracked with it. The smiles built up inside him, R and me smiling madly into his face until it couldn't hold any more. It cracked and out came his smile, urgent, almost demented.

Almost, I say, because he catches my eye like a real smiler, like the first person who learnt to smile. Or cracked with it.

R meanwhile has learnt not to smile. The smiles have sunk down further than we can see. He has also stopped hammering.

* * *

In the ancient times the ocean rose until it covered everything in sight. It covered the trees and the beasts and even the mountains, and ice drifted over their tops.

* * *

Now I have N to baby, as well as Z, and R stays under the duvet. He does not make his fingers into ducks, even when I use him as a cushion for the baby. He does nothing as Z turns towards him, mouth open, looking for milk or salt.

I take the baby away. He smells like his father.

N can get out of bed, sometimes, and dress himself. He can wash himself, occasionally. He cannot cook. G did all that.

They always had a retro relationship, R used to say. Like a beaded purse or beards or big round glasses. Vintage.

* * *

I do what I can: cook pasta and tip tinned sauce over it. I eat more than I need. If I don't, I might float away. There is only Z holding me to the earth, and he is still so light.

I strap him to my body in the complicated carrier we bought before. He hates it. His body arches like a magic flipping fish.

He insists that I carry him as though I am rescuing him from a fire.

* * *

On the sixth day of all this I go to the garden with a hammer. I look at R's progress but it means nothing to me. I hit one nail and it goes through the wood at an angle. I do it again. It is satisfying, like sex or murder.

Z watches me from his blanket on the grass. He flinches with every bang. I stop.

* * *

N doesn't listen to the news any more. Or watch it. No one does. This is how we don't know for so long. This is how we do it.

There is a channel that only screens talent shows. This is N's favourite now. He turns it on in the morning, when they have the compilations.

Z enjoys the shows too, and I cannot deny there is something moving about them. Person after person, stepping forward and singing as though it mattered. Crying. Begging for mercy.

We start to eat in front of the TV.

* * *

In the first light of dawn, a black cloud grew from the sea. They saw the shape of the storm coming towards them, taking up the whole of the sky.

* * *

R gets up sometime in the third week. He has decided to be a man. He turns off the talent show. N complains, but R throws the cupboards open dramatically and rummages until they look almost empty. He turns on the news.

It is bad, the news. Bad news as it always was, forever, but worse. More relevant. This is what you don't want, we realize. What no one ever wanted: for the news to be relevant.

See? R shouts, pointing at the TV. Z starts to cry, right

on cue. I pick him up and jiggle him. I whisper-sing in his ear.

* * *

Panic. Crush. G. Panicked. Crushed.

* * *

Z likes it when I sing pop songs, lively ditties about dancing and broken hearts.

Just before he was born, there was a tune everywhere. It wafted from summer cars, steamed from the pavement, snapped out of cereal.

I hum the tune into Z's balloon cheek: he remembers, I am sure.

We dance. My hands under his loose armpits, his unfocused eyes meeting mine, rolling away.

* * *

Full of him, I used to take the train to work. The tune trailed over my domed self, budded into my ears.

They never announced the platform until the last possible moment. I focused on details to make time go faster; a man's arm hair wisping from under his watch strap, the crocodile gleam of a woman's green shoes.

When the number came we arrowed onwards, aimed ahead of each other, all the details lost in the push.

Once, someone knocked me over. An accident, I presumed. He didn't look back.

* * *

We sleep together now. Every time taking care not to squash the baby, not to suffocate him under our dreams.

At night, more words surge out of R. His version of news fills the square room, the light around the curtains.

The crowds flatten the pillow, they crush the sheets into the crest of a wave. They carry the night away, hour by hour.

When R shouts, Z turns, his downy brow wrinkled towards the noise.

* * *

In the mornings, R has replaced hammering with digging.

We are growing our own vegetables, we are dig-for-victory, we are eco-sustainable heroes.

We live on tinned food, and we wait.

*   *   *

The water rose and rose, and they could not recognize each other in the torrent, in the endless rain from above.

*   *   *

The vegetables are still seeds. The cupboards reveal themselves more by the day: their wooden backs, the greying corners we never used to see.

And yes, R goes with N to get food.

R wants to leave N here, but N insists. And yes I scream and hold their clothes and tell them not to go. And yes they go.

*   *   *

On our third day alone Z laughs for the first time. I am leaning over him, singing an emotionally confused song about his father and grandfather.

And Z cracks his empty mouth open and out it comes as though it has been brewing for weeks: a tremendous cackle. The upsurge of the genuinely amused.

And I put his head against my head and smell the point just above his ear, the smell that makes me want to eat him.

*   *   *

We watch the talent show channel for two to three hours a day. We watch the earth, as though it might suddenly sprout vegetable matter. We watch the drive, in case it sprouts a car.

*   *   *

I carry on with the skin to skin, like the midwives showed me, stripping our two bodies in the silent midday sun, letting the bed sheets hold us, letting the chemicals work.

It is true I am filled with a certain calm. Bovine or not, I cannot tell.

It is true that he moves his mouth to the nipple with a skill seen nowhere else. He still jerks his limbs without control. He is doubly incontinent.

And yet – here is his serious reaching, his controlled opening and sucking and swallowing.

It seems that he is feeding me, filling me with a steady, orange light.

* * *

This is how his body curls: like a shrimp, like a spring, like a tiny human yet to straighten out.

One day we are looking for the talent shows and we flick past the news, like catching a glass on the edge of the sink with your sleeve. That is a good one. It is just like that, all the smashed glass on the floor, all the pieces of what we knew laid out in front of us. Sharp.

I flick the channel onwards, sweep it away before it can cut us: the quickness, the confusion, the way dead people's feet stick up like that under sheets, as though giving a final salute.

* * *

I have come to admit that I love the smell of his nappies. There is little else to love here, or everything. The way the kitchen table shines when I have cleaned it.

The earth that R turned. Recently disturbed.

Z loves milk so much it sends him into a stupor. He falls back from my breast like a drunk.

* * *

Every beast perished, every moving thing. Only one man and one woman survived on the waters, their bodies kept in a wooden box.

* * *

Once: the smell of G's wardrobe, of light through slats and moth wings, I imagine. Of tented skirts Z and I could lie beneath.

Twice: G's mascara on the sink, in the sculpted well for the soap. It rolls there, slightly.

* * *

When I met her for the first time, G hooked me by the elbow. She squeezed my fingers until they hurt.

She spoke words onto my shoulder, thanked me, said pleased, said R.

Her breath was salmon caught leagues away. Salmon smoked over oak, like it says on the packet. Hanging there, in a cabin in the woods, I thought.

Hanging for days, for weeks or months, until it changed.

* * *

On the talent shows, they torture the contestants. They pretend they are rejected, dangle them by their ankles above the abyss. Then, with a sharp tug, they are back in the sun. Glorious. The elation.

All of them still ten years, eight years, three years away from all this.

* * *

I try not to listen for the engine, for the way it will hum through me like a heartbeat. This means I listen constantly. Through the 10,000th rendition of 'I Will Always Love You'. Through Z's breath: heavier now, more solidly alive.

I no longer worry about crushing him in my sleep. I sleep like a shark, swimming on through the night. Never stopping the movement, quick as fins in the dark, between complete terror and complete devotion.

This is the closest I have come to bravery.

* * *

The mountains were covered, and every land under the heavens, and nothing moved there.

* * *

There are so many different kinds of quiet, and only one word for them. The quiet in the house has matured from quiet as lack of noise to something else, a textured, grainy quiet, a thickness to stumble through.

Z seems to sense the shift: he no longer cries when he wakes, as though the quiet were lying on his mouth, a thick blanket.

Or perhaps this would have happened anyway. Consciousness is no longer a shock.

He wakes to my sour breath on his cheek: I wonder what this is to him, this shark vapour, the nightly turning of my jaw.

* * *

R told me to stay here.

* * *

As for food, I have started to think of it all as milk.

Tinned potatoes suspended like specimens and lentils in smooth beads through my hands, frozen fingers of sausages and scurrying rice: all of these are nothing but milk.

I taste it: it is sweet and thin. It billows from me like winter smoke in the bath.

For now, there is an excess, a honeyed pain as it rises through me. Sometimes, when Z pulls his mouth away, it arcs a foot in the air, a white fountain that falls on his nose, his chin, his eyelids.

I wonder how long we would survive, how quickly human milk runs out in famine. I itch to google.

* * *

A dove was sent to see if the water had left the face of the land, but she found no place for her foot.

* * *

Memories are starting to leak: the faint, perfumed waft of the photocopier in my office. The cold room filled with machines, the small window, like a cloister.

The bones under the skin of R's hands when he played the piano, their crackling, their quick moves like spiders.

The first sip of an iced margarita, its meeting with tongue, throat, chest. The moment of a swallow: so final, so decisive.

These are the remains of a life, it seems. The un-savoured, the savoured.

Days are thin now, stretched so much that time pours through them.

Yesterday, like today, I had a full stomach. My breasts were hard or soft, a kind of clock of their own.

Now, without Internet, without phone reception, there is this: the filling, the emptying. The lumpiness of an engorged breast. The tingling of its release. There is this.

iv.

The car arrives when I am not watching or listening. I am asleep in the soaking light of our bedroom, with Z sprawled on my belly, snuffling into motherflesh. We are beasts in the sun. We are, for seconds, oblivious.

R is in the room like a man with a machine gun in a teenage bedroom in the middle of the night. He has no gun but somehow this is what he is like. I think I saw this in a film.

He is shouting that we have to leave, now.

I am nap-blank; I have forgotten. R's words move in and out of focus. Something is nearly happening, he seems to be saying.

Z lifts his head, a heroic effort. He does not cry, but regards his father as you would a fly: curious, irrelevant.

* * *

In the car I realize I have no nappies. The stacked supply in the cupboard that grew shorter every day, like a reverse child. I have left it behind.

Nappies, I say to Z *sotto voce*. He is squashed against me froggily, the seat belt wrapped over his shoulders.

I imagine the curdy shit flowing through his clothes, gathering in my crotch as we drive.

They're in the back, R manages through the grip of his mouth. He is driving the car like a tank.

I turn my neck. The whole back seat is filled with tins stacked in wholesale rows of three. At the edge I spot the optimistic colours of nappy packaging, a glimpse of a cartoon giraffe's neck.

R is yellow-white. He is wearing the same clothes he was wearing when he left two weeks ago. I don't ask him.

* * *

We see no cars for a while, but that is almost normal here.

Z falls asleep, his spell-breath pulling me down. Every time we see a car R flinches. There is rain, and the noise of the wipers, and that is it. Some of the road lights still work; their colours seem antique.

* * *

When I wake up R is sitting straighter and there is a tiny rub of pink on his cheeks.

We're over the border, he says, and smiles. The words are a gap, a meaning distance I can't cross.

I can see people by the roadside, walking in groups. Like mass hitchhiking with no lifts. Some have children balanced on their shoulders. Some are limping.

Their clothes are covered with bright, smart water-proof jackets bought for Sunday walks. Orange, purple, turquoise. They stick out of the gloaming like flags.

* * *

We sleep in the car, somehow, our seats reclined, R's fingers draped over the gearstick. Sometimes our hands touch.

Z just has to move his mouth down slightly and I slide the nipple in. He grunts happily. He needs nothing more.

I have been an orphan for ten years. Neither of us have any siblings.

The window is completely black, the darkness total. We are the only people here. The truth: we've always felt like this.

* * *

From a handful of clay he was made, and she was made after him. They were placed in a cave, and told to fill the world with children.

* * *

When R asked me to marry him we were at the centre of the earth. The guide took us to a line on the ground. He showed us how water ran down a funnel in one direction on one side of the line, and in the opposite direction on the other.

I found this hard to believe.

Once we were alone, R started rummaging. He thought it was a good spot, a good story.

I realized this was one of the tucked moments I'd forgotten about: the proposal. I wondered how I'd remember it: the strange, clear heat of the equator, R's face rounding up at me like a souvenir.

* * *

It is colder up here, and living in a car makes me ache.

R is afraid of the official facilities, the churches and schools lined with mattresses. He doesn't trust the camps, the white tarpaulins that billow at us from fields.

We have everything we need, he says. He carries Z around and my arms feel light, almost floating.

At school we used to hold each other's arms down for so long they would drift upwards when we let go.

Once I tied a piece of string around my finger until it turned red, then blue.

* * *

When Z is down for the night, nestled in blankets in the back of the car, we light a fire in the scrub. R uses his boy-scout skills and I pretend to learn them.

It is now that I ask R about N, and put his heavy wet head in my lap. He tells me how it happened. How quick things became.

I touch his curls, relics from somewhere far off. R's charmed curls, his toddler-smile. None of it worked.

I can see every star in the sky. They look straight through us, a sparkling indifference.

The words lodge in R's throat, in his chest, in the joints of his fingers. He couldn't stop it. His hand shakes, gently, against my leg.

Nowadays, these things can happen in two minutes. They can happen in two seconds.

It turns out that G was right in a way, about the war. I never gave her any credit.

* * *

Here are some of R's words for what happened: tussle, squabble, slaughter.

R has N's watch, he tells me. He has it somewhere. He doesn't put it on.

* * *

Z develops a cold. His very first illness. R says fresh air will clear it up. He takes him for long walks in his arms.

Back at the car, I rearrange the tins.

* * *

N is not gone from here. He would never have been here, with damp bark in the morning. The grass is wet, waiting for our shoes.

N would raise his wide rear from the sofa and let out rippling farts. Unembarrassed, it seemed. Like Z. Free with himself.

R misses him from somewhere else. From when N lifted him up and threw him in the air. From the moment of the catch.

* * *

I hover over Z, looking for signs of stopping. His breath is on-off, like it was after his birth. He is full of thick liquid.

* * *

Man was formed from dust, and the air of life was breathed into his nostrils. It spread through his body until he took a breath, and became a living being.

* * *

One night Z sounds like a rasping old woman or a tiny dog. A memory from a baby advice book, something about the bark of a seal. I have never heard a seal bark, but this could be it.

When Z was born he got stuck for hours, but on the last push he came out all at once, like a seal on a wave.

He is still growing. His toes strain against the cloth feet of his babygrows. I cut through the fabric with a bread knife. He wears them with socks.

* * *

In his second poorly week Z stops drinking my milk. He turns away from the softness as though he is tired of it. He sleeps all day. At night, he is still a seal.

* * *

In the dark, I tell R what we have to do. When I tell him in daylight he shakes and turns yellow-white again. He wants to stay away from people, always.

I am hoping my voice in his ear will work like hypnosis. All night I do it, leaning across the car until my back hurts and he pushes me lightly away.

* * *

In the morning, things speed up. Z's lips turn slightly blue at the edges. His eyes close with a resolution I haven't seen before.

R drives at a hundred miles an hour.

V.

We are back in a hospital, thousands of miles and thousands of years away.

The years stretch forward or back, it isn't clear. The hospital is just a white roof, large rooms with beds and chairs and people spilling out at the edges.

R faints when we see the crowds. He has become allergic.

The doctors think he is the emergency. Thin, shining R. But I say no no and push Z into their arms.

They react. I am unsure, I realize, if they do this any more. If a baby is still something. It is. They react.

* * *

R is told he cannot sleep here. He is relieved.

At night I stare at the blank ceiling until my eyes win and I let them close. I do not miss the stars.

They have injected Z, which made him sob with some vast, rare sorrow. But now his breathing is happening again, and the old woman and tiny dog and seal have gone away.

* * *

The child was born from a golden egg. When the egg split in two, the halves became everything: the heavens and the earth.

* * *

Only one night, we are told. Z's lips are red and he drops onto the breast, a resurrected creature.

We are back in the car, in the never-ending journey that has become our life. It is cold. Z coughs, just once.

Enough, I tell R, and he stops the car.

* * *

He has not researched the best camp. He has not spent hours poring over comparative reviews of refugee camps. He wants none of them.

So we stop next to the first one we see after I say enough. After the crying and the mess of logical statements, punctuated by Z's snores.

We arrive tear-thirsty, with a car full of tins. R says we will be mugged.

But they have medics here, and beds, and heaters, and winter is coming, I say.

These are our boring statements, back and forth into hours of thinning time.

This is how we make it to Shelter 26, with its camp beds and cot. Its blankets and smells of wet dog and grass. Three meals served, day after day after day.

* * *

R lasts much longer than I expect. By the time he leaves, Z has learnt to hold things.

* * *

Everything was made from the soil of the earth. Tree, ox, human. Out of pity they were given warmth, and told to be kind and good.

* * *

Z stares at the things put close to him. Keys, a tooth-brush. A toy provided by a charity – a cloth boy emerging from a cloth banana. Z stares and his voice gurgles through his chest. His eyes flash with frustration.

Go on, my boy, R coos, holding the toy close enough for Z to reach. I think of the complicated Baby Play System I bought when I was pregnant, all its attachments floating free in the rooms of our flat.

* * *

One day he makes it: he forms his fist with the necessary power and is holding the cloth banana, triumphant. The cloth boy dangles out, helpless.

* * *

Z and I can tolerate the camp. I went to boarding school. He is sixteen weeks old.

There are rules and rotas and porridge daily: very Scottish. There is even a baby and toddler group, held in Shelter 4 every Wednesday. I have not known the day of the week for ages, but here it is displayed outside the catering tent every morning.

I try to feel the solidity of the date beneath me, try to make the day and the month and the year mean something.

It is never quiet here. Z learns to cry loudly again. He is not the only one.

* * *

R drives away on a sunny day, the day it is our job to help with breakfast. He has not been sleeping. He eats like a feral cat I once had, stealing scraps to hunch over in the corner.

G and N.

The calamity, and the further calamity – disasters breed like rabbits – and now this, crowded by strangers every long hour.

I count the reasons.

* * *

He says it will only be for a week or so. To get a break.
To look into other options.

He says we should stay, that it is safer. The relief is
hanging from him, a loose shirt.

I look at the car before I lose it. I try to take in all of its
details.

Before he leaves, I put his full hand over my face, like
a mask. I do this even though there is no point. Even
though smells can't be held.

* * *

*The first man and woman met, and became one flesh: they
were naked, and felt no shame.*

* * *

Z is trying to roll over, already. It looks like someone trying to turn over a car with their bare hands.
Impossible.

Sometimes mothers develop superhuman powers when their children are in danger. It is called hysterical strength.

* * *

Z refuses to sleep in his cot. There are only single beds here, so we share one, Z hooped in the arc of my arm or lying splayed on my stomach.

When R leaves people begin to speak to me. Spooning porridge into our mouths, still crusty-eyed and climbing out of dreams. Another woman with a baby on her lap. Brown hair and sunken features. P.

It is hard to get used to listening again. The first few times I hear nothing but a rush in my ears, like holding up a shell.

P asks me about R. I tell her about his time away, and she nods. She lost hers south of the border.

In the disturbances, she says. This is one of the words people use.

Her baby looks grotesquely large to me, with a huge

head and completely erect body. He is eight months old.

* * *

Z wakes up to feed approximately thirty-eight times in the night. I wonder what this can mean.

Every time: a small, fumbling race to his mouth before the scream.

The gasping latch, and his breathing slows in the dark. The world inflates and deflates with him, a giant bellows.

Out: to the hills that surround our squared camp. To the border. To whatever is left.

In: past the dampening tent. Past each bulked mound around us, each collection of breath.

* * *

I have noticed that P sits with a group of other women at lunchtime. They all have babies.

48

In London mothers formed into clubs when pregnant, then marched around in their groups after the birth, swerving their pneumatic buggies around our feet.

I would never be like them, I promised myself.

* * *

When I was four or five my neighbour and I filled water bombs and adopted them as our children.

We stroked their transparent blue or green stomachs. Gave them names and wrapped them in hand towels. Drew faces on, two eyes and a semicircle.

* * *

I go and sit with them. They are the husbandless. They are the milk drippers, the exhausted ones, with hair streaked with grey and rips in the knees of their jeans.

Z bares his gums and waves a teaspoon around. This is the extremity of his social aptitude.

O, a woman with a large, kind-looking nose, is almost hit by the spoon. She doesn't mind.

How old is he? she asks, and this is how it begins.

* * *

At the toddler group there are more toys than Z has ever seen in his life. He seems delighted, gurning over the colours and shapes, hauling everything towards the abyss of his mouth.

I am giving him a normal childhood, I think to myself.

* * *

They start to make the porridge with water. There is no milk to add. We know better than to complain, but it is oddly close to gruel, to the stuff I shoved at my classmates on Victorians Day.

Lunch becomes a thin soup. One slice of bread each.

The only real meal comes in the evening.

At night, my stomach reaches up to ask for more.

* * *

Bye, Baby Bunting, Daddy's gone a-hunting, I sing to Z.

I imagine R alone on the beach in front of a newly raised-up, swirling sea. People say they can sense when a missing person is still alive, and I try this with all my might.

* * *

The first one's bones were made of branches, his blood of rivers, his eyes of moons, his spirit of fire.

* * *

People have started to leave, packing their bags quietly, as though no one will notice. This should mean more for us, but others arrive daily, filling the shelters with their breath and pains.

* * *

When I was six the neighbour's goat had kids. Two of them, delicately different, with tiny, chalky horns and wobbling legs. The neighbour girl and I gave them bottles.

Or that's what I remember, anyway. Tucking the rubber teat between the long, hairy lips. Trying to look into button-slit eyes.

* * *

One day Z finally does it. I have placed him on the bed for three minutes while I put our things away. Nothing can be left out here.

He chooses these three minutes, from all the minutes of our life, to master his latest milestone.

He flips off the bed and onto the floor, crushing his triumph under a wall of crying, a never-ending hurling of his disappointment at the universe.

I am a terrible mother, I think, nestling his unbroken body into my own. P comes, and O, and they tell me no. It happens to everyone.

* * *

The lone lines on pregnancy tests looked like failure, a singular plainness.

I thought I was pregnant every single time. I would test the soreness of my breasts with the tops of my arms at work, squeezing them as I typed.

One month, the faintest of lines on a supermarket test. Then, days later, the blood, like a sickness, a burial.

I mourned it, kept one hand over my fruitless middle.

* * *

After the eighth cycle of hope and weeping into R's silent chest I went online. I needed my people, the other ones. I found them in forums with purple font on a pink background.

I found the stories I needed. I found a new language. The day mrsjackal79 got her BFP (Big Fat Positive). She had cooked a casserole. She had gas. A stronger sense of smell. I stalked through these pretty narratives, looking for my own symptoms.

I longed for these women's kitchens. For their American hobbies, their deep-fried chicken and quilts. These women drove big cars. They had big husbands who were trying to impregnate them. They were succeeding.

* * *

People I know start to leave. P leaves. She says there is a better camp, with more food, forty miles north. She has been offered a lift.

O does not leave. She moves into our shelter, five beds away.

Her baby, C, is the same age as Z. We pretend they are interested in each other.

* * *

After the twenty-fourth cycle of faux-nausea, of imagining the taste of coins and kicks like butterfly wings, R agreed to see a doctor.

The doctor told us we had little hope, without donors, operations, pumpings of drugs.

The next month, I had no symptoms. When my period was two weeks late, I took a test: hopelessly, casually, with professional ease.

The second line showed immediately, like a voice out loud.

* * *

I cannot leave, I tell O. I have to wait for R.

The first properly cold night. I cover Z with breath all the way through. Hot potatoes.

Then, some news. An actual announcement in the catering tent. I drop a small amount of porridge on Z's head. He doesn't seem to notice.

* * *

We are told not to panic, the most panic-inducing instruction known to man.

The quiet packers turn into noisy packers. Into evangelical packers.

I overhear clippings, confused whispers: incursion, interruption, increase. A quickness over the hill, the hills turned quick, coming towards us.

We are too close to the border here, O says. She and C have the same expression, all pursed lips and eyes thick with something I can't work out.

* * *

When I was pregnant I kept expecting it to drop out of me, to fall into the shaking waters of a public toilet, or just slide down my trousers one day at work.

It wasn't until I was lumbering with it, cowboy-legged, that I believed in a baby.

* * *

There are buses to take us further north, if we want. Village buses, with fuzzy multi-coloured seats.

I search for the car the whole way there. I think, if I see R, I will jump from the bus and wave my arms.

This is a bad plan, but I have nothing else. Z and C sleep. O stares out of the window until her eyes shut themselves.

She flickers through her dreams in a way I recognize.

We have learnt to stay half awake, like horses sleeping standing up. Hysterical strength.

I watch. Not a single car passes by.

vi.

In the mornings the sun comes in like any other day. O tells me to remember: the sun has no idea what happened.

She finds this reassuring. I don't.

I find O reassuring, with her hook nose, her round hips. She has kept those, when everywhere people have started to look like models, all visible angles.

They are envied, those hips, and somehow hopeful: a sign of the past among us.

O has ideas too, not just hips, and she pours them into my ear when it gets dark.

This is what I sensed in her: plan-making, strategy. It makes her blood like syrup, slow with all the thoughts.

She is like R in this way. I lace my fingers in hers and tell her no. Good ideas, but no.

* * *

The fifth world is a place you cannot imagine, reached through the bubbles of the first lake. We will all be led there – not yet, but tomorrow.

* * *

Me, Z, O, C. We half-sleep in a row, the babies suckered onto our nipples. They are six months old.

They have learnt to sit up here, in this place of not-enough. They have straightened their backs. They have started to grab at our bread.

* * *

We have possibly come too far for R to find us. Across valleys, up hills covered in trees. But maybe he can plot our route, like a child's pirate map, from there to here. Small red dashes.

Here is the poor relation of there, with facilities so basic we laugh at our previous ignorant luck. Maybe this will be the way it goes, from now. Every few months fresh knowledge of the past, of how good it was compared to the present.

What shall I say? It is dull-cold. This has become one thing, the chill and the boredom seeping into everything, invisible and everywhere.

It is enough for us to be intact, we realize. To have all of our limbs. To be conscious. To still have milk in our breasts.

* * *

We have made a discovery: the maths is in our favour.

I can stay with both babies, and O can queue with her old donated toothbrush, her allocated disc of soap.

I wipe bottoms times two, I keep tiny things from four hands, I play games with twenty puffed toes.

* * *

We put the babies on a blanket together and lower our faces into theirs. We sing to them until someone tells us to shut the fuck up.

We take their nappies off and let them kick, their legs like cloth in old paintings, every fold as clear and stark as a line of ink.

There is nothing but this, their small bodies, time sliding now, losing form, turning one day into the next.

* * *

We talk through it. We pass our stories like spare change.

O used to be an English teacher in Surrey. She was separated from her partner quickly, in the first few weeks. She has nearly always been a single mother.

I tell her about R, whose eyes have arrived in Z's head. I tell her how we met, how quickly we fell into bed.

I find myself wanting to give her the details: how delicious his mouth was to me, like sweets. The hollow in his chest that gave just enough space for a head to rest.

O points out that I am using the past tense.

* * *

We leave on a grey morning when the children have caught irritation from each other like a disease. They gnaw on their fingers. They squirm against our arms. They drip clear, stretchy fluid from their mouths.

* * *

Two men – D and L – are setting off, and O tells me we are going too. Golden opportunity, she sells me. The chance of petrol.

We are inches from them, these strange D and L men. I have another plan, involving grabbing the steering wheel.

Their skin is outside-raw and sore-looking, with straggling beards growing into patches of red. Compared to Z's silken orb cheeks they look fifty years old, but they are young.

They joke with each other like five-year-olds, the tic of nerves familiar beneath each jibe.

O thinks the babies make us non-women, as far as these men are concerned. She thinks they make us safe.

*   *   *

Somewhere towards the base D's neck looks soft. He tells us about his life before.

I was in advertising, he says. We are used to these terms, to the young using the language of the retired.

He talks about the crazy commute and the guys, the nights out and the return to his flat, quiet and waiting for him.

His words take form in the landscape we pass, wrap themselves like gauze around trees, settle on abandoned houses, new cobwebs.

A checkpoint.

How easily we have got used to it all, as though we knew what was coming all along.

*   *   *

A secret: I thought having a baby would stop the fear.

When I was a child, my mother told me she would die for me, of course.

I asked her all the time. Tested her.

The fear of ending woke me up, it choked me. It rendered me incapable. I thought a baby would stop it. Give me something to die for.

* * *

I want to write about the checkpoint quickly. Get it over with.

Theyforceusoutofthecarbabieswillmakeussafedoesn'tse emtruetheyareroughwithusandtheysearchustheymakeu stakeourclothesoff.

* * *

The young men are boys, I see now. Their skin is bright white in the wind.

* * *

Then they saw an angel standing in the light of the sun with his arms outstretched. He called to all the birds that fly, and they came.

* * *

We stop for the night at an empty house. We all sleep in one room without even thinking about it.

We do not want to explore, to look through the drawers of someone who has fled.

We do not want to imagine the fleeing, or the reasons why.

In twenty-four hours, I have started to love D and L. They sleep deeply.

* * *

We don't tell them about the boat until the last possible moment. It is O's information, her possession, a friend of hers from teacher training college.

Contacts, networking, people who might do it. Share.

* * *

O and I have started knowing each other's thoughts. She thinks it is coming through the milk.

Sometimes I sleep with both babies, a twin-mum, turning from one side to the other. Their sucks are almost identical.

C used to do it harder, before we all started to smell the same.

* * *

I am not sure if R would approve. I do not know where he would approve from, or if approving still exists.

He is in another dimension, is all I can think. A pixelated world, perhaps. Or a galaxy of blue-black, floating slowly out to space.

* * *

When I was a child we had knives in a row, lightly stuck to a magnetic strip on the kitchen wall. A gash in the linoleum where one fell, once.

I wondered if I would clamber for the knives, without knowing it. If I might do it in my sleep.

I wondered if I might put one into myself, in the smother of night, in the huge dark space that followed bedtime.

* * *

We ask D and L to drive us to the coast, and for a day or two it is close to something like a holiday. A Scottish holiday, with a rushing sea and the sky filled with clouds dense as drapery.

The beaches are empty, of course. We remember that this used to be a good thing.

* * *

I have read that, when someone knows they are going to die, the world becomes acutely itself.

* * *

Z likes it when L holds him under his arms, his round belly bulging out like a friar. He digs his toes into the sand and lights his smile into me. He bounces as though the earth were made of rubber.

* * *

This is the place for the ones who have died in rain, or lightning, or from diseases of the skin. It is a place of flowers, and of dancing.

* * *

Telling them is O's idea. She is better than me.

They have given us a share of their food. We had a little to add, all the way back from R's stash. But mainly we have taken.

We are four now, truly, the babies eating from our plates, gumming cold beans down and letting them swell back up again as we try not to wince at the waste.

It was unclear from the beginning what we added. Baby-flesh as repellent worked. Or L and D are good boys. Definitely this.

So we tell them. But not until we see it coming towards us like an alien craft, the only thing out there, a spot on the endless blank.

* * *

When you have a child, the fear is transferred, my mother could have told me.

In a way, it is multiplied, she could have said.

* * *

D and L do not want to come.

For a rare moment O and I are speechless, each holding the other's baby, splashes of colour on the black and white of sea and sand.

The boat comes as close as it can.

We roll our clothes up and walk in. The sea streams into every part of my head.

C's arms are around my neck. I lower my face to her skin-silk. I breathe it all in.

vii.

The water reminds Z of where he came from.

He is the most comfortable person on the boat, his softness slouching against mine, the rocking motion undulating his cheeks.

The others watch him hungrily, as though they can catch his contentment.

C cannot stand it. She lets her cries stream straight from her mouth to the sea. O has learnt to hold her due south. We can still hear her, but the sound flows behind us this way. Like an engine.

* * *

D and L waved at us until we couldn't see them any more, the only people against the straight lines of earth and tide.

For a few miles, I keep expecting their limbs to surface from the waves, creamy white and searching.

* * *

The sun glares, droops and Z naps, his head tucked under my chin. Soon, we are night sailing.

This is the closest you can get to it: the void, the nothing, the black lapping mouth of the sea and the black arching back of the sky.

The stars seem to mean something now. They are maps.

Z likes the darkness, as well as the water. He opens his eyes into it.

* * *

The otherworld will be beneath the ocean, forty thousand fathoms below. In that place, there will be no pain, nor death, nor mourning.

* * *

The others are H, O's friend from college, his wife F, and their children B and W.

Family trip, O says, clambering across the boat. The children hold on to her legs as though they know her.

They are much, much older than Z. They are a different species. Their limbs are long, like insects, and their eyes are huge, as though they've been stretched by something.

At night, they sleep against their mother; they are too big to melt into her. They prop their hard skulls against her bony shoulder. They bump down and jolt, and then do it again.

* * *

F looks more fearful than us. Her mouth has puckered with it.

* * *

The island is safe, O used to whisper in my ear, all those nights in the camp.

We felt fifty people shift around us, the reality of human smells we kept hidden for so long.

There is none of this there, O would say.

She knew a way to get a message. Knew someone going. Knew someone. The insistence of her hot words in my ear, the yeasty foreign blast of her breath.

* * *

It is safe, H repeats now, his arms pulling on ropes, turning handles, dealing with the endless diversions of cloth and wind and wood. The most complicated machinery I have ever failed to understand.

Safe now. Maybe not forever. He casts the words off the side like pebbles, pats his fingers on the edge of the boat. He has taken to this well. He is tanned. Healthy.

* * *

In that place, honey-sweet fruit will touch your lips with gold. Sunshine will lay you down and bless you, and moonlight will fill your bones.

* * *

We arrive in the morning, in a salty sun starting to break. Z knows something is different. He pushes his arms and legs against me with astonishing force. He wants to be put down.

On the beach he lowers his head, raises his rear like a crab. He lifts his pearly hands up, and shrieks when I stop him filling his mouth with sand.

I hold him over the water. We watch as a wave passes over his shell-skin, washing every grain away in its foamy rush.

* * *

The house was built for this, for the highest sea and the strongest winds the world can make.

From its windows, all you can see is miles and miles of it. The shimmering green-grey-blue terror. Orange in evening, then gone.

* * *

The first night, Z cries through every hour. We are swallowed in his noise.

O and C are in the next room. We have divided here, hidden behind walls that feel like bodies to touch: dense, filled with something.

I hold my breast in my hand like a medieval painting, pushing the nipple towards his clenched mouth.

It is all I have. I am a one-trick mother.

He turns away. He cries himself down for the first time, dragging himself to the unconscious wail by wail. Once he is asleep, I stare at the flushed oblivion of his cheeks.

His crying rings in my ears like a distant alarm, like something I've forgotten, left on by mistake.

* * *

This is the place where snow never falls, where there is no thunder or lightning. All days are silent, and covered in a clear light.

* * *

O sees it before me, sees the new white glint in his mouth, the waiting mound that has finally pushed through. A tooth.

* * *

I cannot see the pirate map any more. I cannot trace R's steps across Z's belly with my fingers in the bath.

Z has a bath now, and a room. He is a real boy, I think. He is no longer a puppet dragged through chaos. He has form.

* * *

Soon I love F, the gentle drape of her sleeve from her arm, the way she leans across to spoon stew onto my plate.

I love the long children too, with their breezy forgetting. I am careful not to love H too much.

I can love O all I want, with her swinging-arm walks on the beach and our babies perched on her hips. One each.

It seems that Z has done something to my heart. Loosened it. Opened up a gap.

* * *

Z and C sit in the bath, their skin reflecting us. The taps drip. It feels like a Sunday.

Z and C sit up, and we watch for falling. They clap their hands together, nearly missing. They tip back. We catch them.

Outside the steamed windows the island continues, its trees rising in the wind, its weather swirling above us, unmoved.

There are ruins everywhere. Remains of other runaways, hundreds or thousands of years ago, H says. Monks, hermits, wild men with bees in their hair.

Now it is almost certainly empty, H tells us. We don't go far, just in case.

* * *

Sleep when they sleep, went the old advice in a book far away and underwater.

But as soon as Z is asleep and the door is closed I am more awake than I have ever been in my life.

The white walls have a friendliness, a pattern of faces, more features every day. There is an old lady close to our bed. She seems to have a beard.

I wonder if I might find R, made of textured paint effects. Or if I can trace him a path to us this way.

When I try to see his face all I get is Z, who pushes his bald head into my neck at night. I wonder if he misses R somewhere in there.

Synapses are electrical messages, didn't they say. Crackling colours like northern lights or deep-sea creatures, floating miles below and right inside us.

* * *

Night speeds by, and we lose it in lamenting. Here comes the place, the right turn, where they all live untouched by sorrow.

* * *

Of course, he likes it when I cover myself in a tea towel, and reappear.

Like my mother reappeared. Like her mother did.

The revelation that something can come back, again. And again. And again.

* * *

We actually grow things here. We put seeds in the ground and they grow. Sometimes. The wind is strong and the soil is something. Too much something.

There is no electricity, but there is the old magic – wood and wick and spark, flames of all sizes.

The taps turn around and around to nothing, but there is a well, with a rope and bucket, like in a nursery rhyme.

* * *

When I wake up in the morning I do not know where I am.

My body registers nothing at this. *Where* doesn't seem to be the question any more.

* * *

I take a rug from the house and put Z on it. We sit in the rough field under the sky, which races away from us towards the happening.

We have arrived at the non-happening, it seems: the

invisible growth of Z's body, the tiny increments of our meals coming out of the soil.

* * *

One night, H gets an old radio working. We hear static, a fruity, post-coital crackle. What was left of the beginning, I heard once.

The mainland is on fire, they say in so many words. After the flood, the fire. I am losing the story. I am forgetting.

I am covered in babies: C and Z are both asleep on me. O is knitting, of all things. The candles thin and fizz. The long children are in bed.

O and I like to imagine our husbands together, on a raft or another island.

Luck is one of those words that has no meaning any more, if it ever did.

Sometimes, I tell myself R is on top of Big Ben. He is clinging to the point.

* * *

One day, I take my clothes off and walk into the sea. I leave O with Z and C, with her eyes on my bare back.

I put my hand over my belly, on my breasts, light for once, drifting in the water like anemones.

When I come out, I am tingling. The cold doesn't leave. It has taken root.

viii.

The transition is gradual, then absolute, like always. One minute Z is scraping in the dirt, his paws scurrying onwards to nothing, like a mole held by the tail.

His middle is so round, so filled with milk and potato and beach and fluff that he seems to have no chance. His wrists are pinkly tender and circled in fat.

* * *

Spring comes in the same way. One day we are seeing our own breath above the bed, my cloud big and diffuse, his small and segmented, like a train.

Then there are flowers poking up in the garden, and Z is crawling.

He defeats the grass, pulls a dandelion so hard it comes

out with the roots attached, flailing like a hello in the breeze.

*   *   *

It is hard to believe that this is only temporary: that Z must progress on, to walking and then running. It seems that this, rather, is another kind of person. The crawling kind.

*   *   *

C is not crawling. She likes to stay in one place, to spread her eyes over her surroundings slowly. It seems then, that she is a different kind. The sitting kind.

*   *   *

How quickly the everyday fills up time again. Glugs upwards from the earth, invisible until you're splashing in it.

It seems it would be like that anywhere. Living on the moon, or hanging upside down from the ceiling, and arguing about teabags and hairs in the bath.

The enraging facts of other people's existence.

* * *

The stars will dim and fade; the fire demons will be led across the rainbow bridge. The enemies will gather on the plain, too terrible to see.

* * *

H rolls up his sleeves at the table. His knees move up and down. Sometimes they wobble our plates. He talks about going to get more people, about rescue missions, refugees, hospitality.

He doesn't go. We all have our own rooms here, and enough food. Stockpiles. We can leave some at the bottom of our bowls.

Here, when Z and C throw food at each other, we don't tell them off, or pick it up from the floor any more, to be rinsed and tried again. We carry on talking.

* * *

Everyone has their theory, their own scratched-out map that helps them into the long days nowhere.

For H it will all be over soon, for O we are here forever.

As for me, I see R in a vessel on the ocean, and then I don't.

It's a mirage, an illusion, a piece of dirt over my cornea.

I blow on Z's belly and he curls his toes. I like the way his fingers stick to me when I carry him, like a bath lizard.

* * *

When I do the washing-up, I turn the radio on. Z crawls around my feet, picking up a spoon, a crust from last night's supper. We listen to the crackle like the wind.

Occasionally, a word gets through. We welcome each one as a friend. I repeat it. Z repeats it, gives his version.

We are learning our own language.

Supper, dignify, project, plan, note, grasslands, plastic, riots, ceasefire, moment, returners, recovery, guidelines, soup.

Some are in bold.

We arrange them in a line, like lottery balls.

* * *

Ceasefire, I say to Z, when I change his nappy. Recovery, I murmur, when I wipe his face, pull a vest over his head.

I think of the fire damped down with tartan picnic blankets.

Ceased with watering cans, cool showers on the flames.

* * *

At work, I used to take minutes. Professor X stated that he thought the Wednesday meat pie was surprisingly inadequate. The incident between a squirrel and cricket spectators was agreed to be unfortunate.

I find myself wondering what the minutes of this would say.

* * *

Often, I am unsure whether something is a bird or a leaf.

* * *

Z likes to eat butter in chunks.

* * *

We are overrun by mice. They leave their droppings in our cutlery drawer, small and brown amongst the steel.

* * *

B and W have become wild children, only returning for meals. Their faces have baked to a crust of sun and dirt.

To keep them in the house for minutes we teach them baby-care skills. F, O, me. Down on our knees, wrapping cloth to make a nappy.

Then we say the secret: there is no skill. There is only another person, smaller than you.

W does a roly-poly as C watches, adoring.

B gets on her hands and crawls with Z. She lifts things and lets them fall. A jumper, a pencil, a potato.

Z yells and his limbs strike out, electrified, his wonder at gravity reaching every part of his body.

* * *

Sometimes, Z sits with O or F and watches my steps. He rocks forward to join me. And I walk five, ten, two hundred feet away.

Then, he is out of sight. He is not-here, a new state of its own.

But still on my fingers: his cheeks, and the soft orange scabs under his hair. A cradle covering, a honeycombed husk.

One day, I leave even this behind, but something remains, at the corners. His shadow, perhaps, a slip of the light. A phantom something, felt more when gone.

* * *

I remember this from early-period R, stepping out of his flat, expecting to re-form, to be one mind in one body.

Then, the taste of him, the dense scented grain of it.

It came from my pores, transferred onto books, handlebars, a coffee cup.

* * *

On the headland, I try a run. I try to make my body into a running shape.

A rabbit passes me, mockingly. A real-life rabbit, like a cartoon. Maybe a hare. And it seems that this is R, all at once, moving, a streak of fawn. Finding his cavity, beneath everything.

The rabbit dives into turf; it disappears. And I lean down, stick my wrist in. Expecting teeth. Expecting the bump of ears against my fingers. Something to capture, to take back.

* * *

The earth will shake, and the mountains will tremble. Some will hide deep in the ground, and the fire will not scorch them there.

* * *

London, I say to Z as he feeds.

I tell him our street name. Our postcode. He reaches into my hair, spins strands around his thumb.

* * *

Often I watch H's hands, the routes he makes with his fingers across his palms. Lifelines.

His children are too tall to carry around, but he holds them upside down, shakes sand from their pockets.

Every morning, he runs around the house, over and over. He comes back damp, hollow, covered in himself.

* * *

One broken night, I open the window, lean over the sky. Z has rolled back into his milk fog, his sleep-breath matching the growls of the sea.

90

I drink fresh air like alcohol, every sip a pulling cool that reaches my waist.

At the straightest edge of the world I think I can see a hulking thickness, a black mark growing. The mainland, I like to think.

It hovers over the water like a boat. It grows, I imagine, blooms rows of houses with lit windows and lives inside. If I squint, I might make out R, waving.

Carried by the waves, he is coming towards us. He is moving away.

ix.

The idea came from nowhere. For weeks it was not there, and then it was everywhere.

It came from the distance, or from sleep, from those nipple head-twist urine-musk times we spend in the dark.

Any chance they get, my dreams unfurl in their allotted small space. They are origami, they are Japanese pod hotels. They fit it all in.

The idea came as a miniaturized image, a crisp packet in the oven. It is all I need.

* * *

Most mornings, I wake with Z's elbow in my eye, his knee on my mouth. Some mornings, his face is above me, a shining son, dribbling.

One morning, we find the world split apart.

The sky has peeled away from the sea, and between them there is only a soft bank of peach, a touchable arcade of light.

Another sunrise.

Z reaches a dumpling finger, makes his sounds.

Towards R, I have to think. R back at the camp, finding archaeological clues, looking for evidence of life.

A shred of cloth banana in the mud, the cloth boy long gone.

* * *

I'll take the boat myself, I say at breakfast, into the jam spreading itself out across the bread.

I imagine Z lying on a sheepskin on deck, wearing a perfectly white babygrow, kicking his legs into salt spray.

I see my hands on the rigging, letting the sails out into knots of wind like sheets.

I can see it, and this means it is possible. This is a fun logic. It makes sense the way the steam from my tea does. Effortlessly.

* * *

Z sees them first: feathers drifting from the sky. First one, then another. Then another, and another.

I call it a sign. I try to catch them.

It's just a bird fight, F tells me. An altercation, way above our heads.

* * *

O doesn't ask me why. She persuades H to take me, tunes in to his rescuing-frequency, to the way he taps out frantic rhythms at mealtimes.

She calls my logic stupid in the friendliest way possible. She uses words like drown.

I say it is pathetic that we are relying on men to transport us around, again. I say it but I do not feel it.

This is how it comes to be, H with his complicated knowledge again, untying ropes. Packing supplies. Making ready.

* * *

O decides to stay. This is the short story.

The minutes would say: after extensive discussion, it was decided that O and C would stay on the island for now with F and H (on his return) and their children B and W. It was agreed that they would attempt to stay in contact with those leaving if possible. It was noted that B and W are unusually self-contained children. It was further noted that they have developed proficiency in infant care.

O tells me she won't say goodbye. She hates goodbyes.

* * *

After the six days and nights of fire all was still, the sea returned to liquid, the earth lying silent beneath the water.

* * *

When we face the whole wet hole of the sea-sky again H and I sit on opposite sides of the boat.

Z clings, a joey in the pouch of my arms. I am almost ashamed to bring him here, to float his small flesh-pocket on the water again. Almost.

I nearly reach for H, for his arms above the fathoms. Nearly.

The thoughts fly off, passing seabirds swirling away.

* * *

Landing. From water to land. From moon to earth.

Or: the beach is the in-between place. The world between worlds, a memory from a book read at bed-time. The rubber taste of my thumb.

It rushes in and out, deserted, soothing. I remember that you shouldn't stay here too long. You can forget everything.

* * *

I half expect D and L to still be here. Perhaps cooking fish over a fire, their skin freckled by the northern light, their hair long, their speech slowed like surfers.

H has moored the boat in a groove, a lapping inlet where he can think of it as hidden.

We don't mention the sail, the blinking white between the rocks.

* * *

We see nothing but abandonment for a long time. We are on foot, passing Z between us like a runaway's bundle, a handkerchief on a stick. Or not, because he wriggles. A rat in a sack.

He wants to crawl, and sometimes we let him. Not for transport, but for rest. We put our large legs out on the grass and he uses our bodies as climbing frames, slides, monkey bars.

* * *

The same checkpoint, a bad joke. This time they are

gentler. No stripping. The same men, I suspect from the corner of my eye, but no stripping.

Maybe it is H, his manner. They call me his wife. He doesn't correct them.

We are in the after. It is tangible, like a smell or a constant background hum.

The sun looks older, orange, sagging, like it might drop. H says it's only mist.

* * *

The same men tell us there are coaches. To take people home.

Home is another word that has lost itself. I try to make it into something, to wrap its sounds around a shape. All I get is the opening of my mouth and its closing, the way my lips press together at the end. Home.

I get Z's lips too, the force of them, their perfect colour. He still has only one tooth.

* * *

We'd heard the change on the radio-wind, but it is a revelation anyway, like the first warm night of the year.

Unthinkable until you open the windows, take your clothes off, sleep under a thin sheet.

* * *

We see our first people. A moment of recognition, a knotted riddle, like passing a minor celebrity in a shopping centre.

I think I know this woman with red curly hair, stained clothes, a face pulled down by exhaustion.

Then I remember: I knew someone with red curly hair, once. Someone else. Somewhere else.

* * *

It seems that people are moving more slowly than before, as though the air means something to them again.

I look for clues in their shirt seams, the grooves of their shoes.

I try to read the sky, to see what the clouds are moving for.

* * *

The earth will rise up from the deep one day, from the surface of the waves. Every land will be empty, and covered in morning dew.

* * *

H may not be rescuing anyone any more. He seems to shorten with this realization, to become less of a protective bulk.

Or maybe it is the coaches that do this, with all their surrounding bustle. The neon jackets of the police may as well be the banners of a carnival.

There is evening light, nearly black, and flashing lights. It's almost like Christmas, I yelp at H, who says nothing.

* * *

Z and I have two seats to ourselves. He presses his cheeks against the window like I used to, making them look vacuum-packed to passers-by, lifting his nose to a snout.

The coach has the same smell of all coaches since the beginning of time. Chemical mixed with nothing.

H stands outside and waves slightly. I wonder when he will go back to the island. I have pressed messages into his brain, told him exactly what to tell O.

I see them scattering, sent across the mystery of H like bottles on waves.

The coach swings around confidently, and I swing with it, looping myself around Z. We are on our way.

Outside the windows, the black is pricked, like the first camera.

Tiny atoms of light shine out from nowhere, reaching for our image, our lit faces, Z's noble chin, my tangled hair.

X.

Whatever I imagine, it is something else.

Where I expect desolation there is the atmosphere of a jumble sale.

Where I envisage welcomes and tea, smiles and Blitz spirit, there is grey concrete, wailing people dragging themselves across the road, photo-boards of the missing.

Our city is here, somewhere, but we are not.

We are all untied, is the thing.

Untethered, floating, drifting, all these things.

And the end, the tether, the re-leash, is not in sight.

* * *

We fill out forms. People have come from nowhere to process our X-marks-the-spot.

I XXX the boxes for flooded-out, for husband-gone, for seeing faces in wall patterns.

I am given coping pills, more forms to fill in about R, and a space in a women-and-children shelter, created from the shell of an insurance company skyscraper.

We are on the eighty-first floor.

* * *

Z is fine or not-fine, is the daily news.

His teeth hurt, goes the excuse, or he needs a crap. He is tired-hungry-angsting, the intricate puzzle, a crossword of causes always left half filled out.

I let him go to the bombproof windows and look down all the way. He doesn't cry.

* * *

The earth was bare, and barren, and no trees grew, and no flowers, and all was still.

* * *

In the daytime, we go for long walks.

We trace the new high-water marks with our eyes. Z smiles at the whole fresh, destroyed place.

It's all background to him, painted cardboard scenery falling over.

* * *

I never realized that bullet holes in buildings were so much like fossils, punctured marks of a prehistoric life. Worm tracks, an infestation.

Constellations of scars. They are brand new, I think, or aeons old.

* * *

We flick through the photos on the found-boards

in double-quick time. We could recognize R just by walking by.

* * *

Up high, at night, I see a face-kaleidoscope, a canopy of features flowering above me.

The missing have thick eyebrows, and thin. They have chins with clefts in. They have blemishes from child-hood mishaps.

I pick out ones I particularly like. I pause them, holo-grams of somewhere else.

* * *

I remember going on a protest when I was fourteen. We sat down in the city's busiest junction. We stopped all the cars until the police or some thugs dragged us away.

Now, the streets are not so much reclaimed as holding their breath. A few of us trail through, the returners, tourists in our own lives.

* * *

In those days, there were people living under the earth.
They began to climb out one by one, holding onto a long,
strong rope.

* * *

Other things we see on our walks: families, men and
women and children who have managed to stay
together.

I want to rush up to them and ask how, but I don't.
Some things are the same.

* * *

I speak to the other mothers in the shelter, but none are
like O.

Plus, Z seems too big. He is always calling me away,
pointing and making sounds that need my ears to make
sense.

* * *

The latest idea for the tourist-returners is boats. I think
I have had enough of boats for forever but these are
different. They will take you across the water to your
place, if it's dry.

Dry is their word.

I go to sign up for the boat to our flat, the place we lived once, I am told. I want to show Z.

If it's really dry, we can resettle, they say. I whisper it into Z's catkin ear, his cool canal. Resettle.

The waiting list is so long we may as well give up, they don't say.

They look at Z as though he is a disability. We leave.

* * *

Communications are down, says the sign in the long hallway.

We know the only way to meet friends is to catch them in the street. To hold your gaze out like netting.

An ear, a cheek. The way someone rubs their nose when no one is looking.

* * *

One day, V from work, caught by the way he picks his nails, his permanent distraction.

He looks like a tramp now, as most of us do.

He doesn't seem to see Z, who reaches for his face, squawks, asserts his reality.

V says things so obvious they almost make no sense.

Behind us, a policeman adjusts his machine gun.

* * *

The people built homes, and made children, and filled the world. But their faces were flat; they had left their joy and sadness behind.

* * *

There are chairs in the insurance company skyscraper. Corporate-type chairs, covered in muted brown fur.

Z's new passion, which he pursues as faithfully as anyone has ever pursued anything, is to put his arms on the chairs and pull his whole self to standing.

The first time he does it, I cheer, raising my fists in the air, squealing in a mother-pitch so high I can hardly hear it.

Z beams, dribbles a fine snail line across the chairs in celebration.

I surprise myself – even now, I still move to tell R, my head turning to the empty space.

* * *

V used to be my boss, sort of. Senior to me. I was his junior all my working days. I often thought of myself as a sort of buffoon.

I left my job behind every day at five, as they say. I peeled it off like a lining.

V never stopped working. I wonder what he does now, now that work is frozen in time. One hand held in the air, one leg lifting from the ground.

* * *

We thought we were like a family. All the lunches we ate together. All the days of sharing air, of letting ourselves out into the same place.

Turns out, there was nothing there.

* * *

Sometimes, too few people in too much space, in squares where Z and I sit alone by fountains with no water.

I could find this funny, all the water in the world, and nothing for a stone cherub to squirt from his tiny penis.

Sometimes, too many people in too small a space. In the skyscraper, every single returner-woman-with-child, it feels like.

Some of these children are teenagers. They roam around trying to kiss or shout their way out.

* * *

I query what the R-equivalent of this place is. I imagine a glinting bank stuffed with men.

I ask the woman who slaps lentils on my plate with a giant spoon.

Z reaches towards the food like a super-baby, arms

straight in front of him, all-in-one suit gleaming red. He is always hungry.

The woman ignores my question. She squeezes Z's cheeks, purses her lips. They gurgle together.

* * *

Most past things are ridiculous now.

Your baby may well be sleeping through the night, the book said, at three months, and six months and nine months.

Sleeping through the night is something no one does any more.

* * *

They went up a large hill and waited for the dawn. They waited for many days, and at last thought they could see the light of the morning star.

* * *

Out of the blue of a long night I remember the name for Z's new moves across the chairs: cruising.

You are cruising now, I whisper to his sleeping heat. He stirs up from the layers, flings an arm across his neck.

* * *

We go to the same square every day for years.

Or: just one very long afternoon, the dark shape of our double-shadow, this life acquiring a deep flavour, a lasting impression.

xi.

The light *has* changed, I think. It is not all just mist.

It changed once before, when I first fell under a boy, like under a bus.

It was that boy who gave light its new jaunty slant, who started the creep of it across tabletops.

* * *

This light is slow rather than sprightly.

It passes over us on bridges, where we stand to pretend nothing has happened. From the best bridge the whole city looks unchanged from most angles.

You can choose whether the buildings are full or not, turn it off and on, like opening and closing an eye, moving an object from left to right.

Yes, I tell Z, when he points.

The buildings are full of people, I tell him. They are on computers. They are doing important things.

Then I tell myself about the emptiness. The rows and rows of desks lined up politely. The paper left in the wrong places.

One piece in the middle of a carpet, a white and square aberration.

* * *

At the start, there was no sun and no moon. She came from a hole in the sky, and fell slowly towards the water.

* * *

I could let Z crawl across the bridges, but then I would have to see it.

His small body, golden cup of a head, turning in the air, hitting the river like an anchor, sinking from view.

The scenarios for his death are the most vivid day-dreams I have ever had.

* * *

I see R's face in the following objects: empty drink cans, rain splash on river, the heads of spoons.

Cars left for dead, each headlight an eye that asks me questions.

* * *

One morning, I realize the new light might be summer.

The skyscraper has no curtains, so every day we are woken with it, this blasting sunshine.

Z wakes immediately, as though sleep was an illusion, an unimaginable blankness.

He comes from sleep as he came from the void: suddenly, without the slightest suggestion of surprise.

* * *

The birds watched her fall from above. She landed beside them, and asked each one to dive for earth.

* * *

This morning, he grapples along the side of the bed like a mountain climber, shows me his gums, an eruption of nubs.

He pushes his fingers into my thighs. I am nothing but material to him, dough for the climb.

* * *

I feed Z, I feed myself. We take turns.

There is a spoon filled with food, and there is its return to his mouth. This is what it feels like: the spoon has always been there, and I am returning it.

When I eat, my stomach stumbles over. It loses its way.

Its turnings remind me of Z, of the way he moved inside me. Some days I felt he would escape that way, that muscle and flesh would be sliced by a toenail.

Pregnancy was the great adventure, it seems now. The great bravery. To allow my lungs to be doubled in size, as it said in the books. To submit to the gulping placenta.

It is only humans and monkeys who let the foetus feed from their own blood supply, I read.

Only humans and monkeys who let their young release themselves back into the mother, float themselves into her, minute explorers.

* * *

Scientists Discover Children's Cells Living in Mothers' Brains, I read, over a bowl of plain rice.

Z squirmed, some hard part of him nudging my hip.

I expected the next article to detail the child found spread across the mother's brain, a sealed film, a complete covering.

* * *

The birds dived again and again beneath the water, look-ing for a piece of earth.

* * *

It comes in a letter form. I think it has been written on a typewriter. It is nearly a telegram.

R has been found. In Medical Shelter 73A.

I stare at the paper and forget the words and remember them. It seems like they are growing in my brain, that cells of this news will stay there always.

* * *

Z has started to let go. For one or two seconds, he stands tall on his own two legs.

This sight gathers up my breath. It takes me like a graze, a sudden rip in the air.

* * *

Medical Shelter 73A starts to curl at the sides of my

vision. It sits on my tongue like a piece of chewing gum I am trying not to swallow.

All I can picture for minutes at a time is men with bandages wrapping their heads, plaster-encased legs hoisted to the ceiling.

* * *

Dadadadadadadadadada, Z says now. He can stand for two seconds, then three.

* * *

The easiest way is to walk, so I put Z on my shoulders (an innovation) and we do the strewn-empty mile or two.

Z pulls on my hairs, sometimes. Every step takes forever.

* * *

Reunions come from television. From sparkling screens edging backwards at the press of a button. Purple, maybe. Glittery, textured.

From the boom of a presenter calling out the names. From the crush of shoulder against cheek under studio lights.

From that one brightly lit ecstasy, skin on skin, distance and separation flattened by the everlasting instant.

* * *

This is how it really is: seconds of almost nothing, edging readjustment to an old face.

Squeezing past each other's words like customers in a too-small shop.

Polite apologies, and all that lives beneath them.

* * *

Weeks and months have gathered in his skin, making it thicker, maybe. Moving his nose one millimetre to the left.

I try to name the difference, give it a word or two. This will help.

I try not to remember his old full-face smile, lasting all the way back to his baby pictures, folded corners in a drawer.

Late summer in the garden, the bath, lamp-grinning out of every single school photograph.

* * *

I think of putting his palm over my face, again.

I try to hold him with my hands, to not squeeze too hard.

I think of the rabbit – or was it a hare? – its quick eyes, its heart thrumming under its fur.

* * *

R will be able to leave soon, the nurses tell me. The key is the afterplan, they keep saying.

I leap on that, but it seems that the afterplan is me. I am what they have been waiting for.

* * *

R is in bed, but that is just for effect. The problem is far from sheets and pillows, wool blankets that scratch.

It is nowhere, and everywhere, and still lodged in his throat. He swallows it down.

* * *

I tell R that we are on the dry list. I say the word home, that old lip-press, and this seems to make him happy. The difference between happy and not-happy is a jerk of his cheek, something like a twitch.

Until. I put our huge boy beside him, and Z puts his face all the way in.

R holds Z's upright body, his transformed self.

They touch noses. Eskimo kiss, goes a phrase from long ago.

Perhaps this is reunion, or the beginning of it.

xii.

We are on boat number 34. Everything has numbers now. R looks for patterns, and I encourage him not to. This is the afterplan.

Z is not showing his father how good he is on boats. He seems to sense the shallowness beneath us, the threatened scrape.

The waters are greyer than I was expecting.

Z bangs his head on my chest.

He reaches into my dress for my breasts. R looks away.

*   *   *

The birds dived for earth, but none could find a single piece.

*   *   *

We have brought all of our personal belongings, like the leaflet tells us to. Everything fits in one plastic bag.

R's donated T-shirt is in there, a pair of boxers wrapped around Z's socks.

He lost everything, he says. Or it was stolen, I imagine. I want to stop imagining.

* * *

I ponder the tone of the leaflet, its early-reader simplicity. Do not hope too much, it warns.

Z improves as we get closer. He stands on my knees, puts his eyes to the horizon like a lookout. I am held by his velvet grip, feel his whole weight quivering, his head above mine.

* * *

Our flat is on the top floor. This is how it is already dry.

The rooms feel like home on a school day. Unused, waiting.

Other returns cluster in the air like dust. Coming back from work, from holiday. The slight refreshment of a change.

* * *

Amongst the ruined old, the sogs of stuff, there is something new, a spreading blotch, a mural of mould.

I think I can see R's absent months there, in scene after scene, white and blue as willow china. This is not the afterplan.

R running. R in hiding, watching it all unfold beneath him.

* * *

In the kitchen: a deep indigo spread. I touch its collapsing centre, its valleys and plains, the borders bumping under my skin.

I move my hand along the trails of the stained wall, veined water paths plotting all the days we missed.

* * *

I walk into the nursery, a room that has never been used for this purpose. The walls are yellow – we didn't know Z was a boy – the pale of the inside of a lemon.

I almost put him in his cot, for the first time, almost let his feet sink into the sponge-sodden organic mattress.

But here is the pattern again, telling the story of R, of every single place he found to hide.

*   *   *

One bird brought earth from the very bottom, caught in its beak like gold.

*   *   *

R is in our room, picking things up one by one and dropping them again.

I touch only his fingers, his large hands that can play the piano.

We have this touch, our fingers in the ruined room, the new slow light drifting around us, our child squirming in my arms.

*   *   *

The earth spread until it became the mountains and fields,
until it became the whole of the world.

* * *

I let Z down on the bare damp boards, on the rotting
wood that glowed a year ago.

He grapples around our knees for a few minutes, feels
his way over the idea of his parents.

Then, he lets go.

His body stands on its two points. He puts his hands up
for balance.

He lifts a leg and – impossible, impossible – he takes a
step.

Thank you

Tim Hunter, for remembering when I had forgotten; Leo and Sylvie Hunter, for making it new; Penny Morris and Ernie Dalton, for understanding, for everything; Kaddy Benyon, for invaluable mentoring, gin, for KEEP GOING; Suzanne Draper, for the labour story; Sophie Hunter, for setting an example, for words in spring 2013 and autumn 2015; Belinda Drake, for electric enthusiasm and all; Madeleine Dunnigan, for making a crucial connection; Laurence Laluyaux, Stephen Edwards, Tristan Kendrick and all at Rogers, Coleridge and White, for guiding the novel on its first journeys; Paul Baggaley, Camilla Elworthy, and all at my publishers Picador, Grove Atlantic, Gallimard, C.H. Beck, Hollands Diep, and Elsinore for big faith in a small book; wonder trio of editors Sophie Jonathan, Elisabeth Schmitz and Katie Raissian, for passion, precision, so much more; brilliant agent Emma Paterson, for insight, generosity, for believing in the end from the start.

* * *

The sections in italics are inspired by and adapted from a myriad of mythological and religious texts from around the world. I am grateful for the inspiration provided by the anthology *Beginnings: Creation Myths of the World*, edited by Penelope Farmer and illustrated by Antonio Frasconi (Chatto & Windus, 1978).